Chichi and the Termites

Wendy Ijioma

MACMILLAN

First published 1992

Published by THE MACMILLAN PRESS LTD
London and Basingstoke
*Associated companies and representatives in Accra,
Auckland, Delhi, Dublin, Gaborone, Hamburg, Harare,
Hong Kong, Kuala Lumpur, Lagos, Manzini, Melbourne,
Mexico City, Nairobi, New York, Singapore, Tokyo.*

ISBN 0-333-57696-9

Printed in Hong Kong

A catalogue record for this book is available from the
British Library.

Illustrations by Gay Galsworthy

'Where's Chichi?' Mother asked. Why did she ask? Chichi was always in the field behind their house, among the caterpillars and grasshoppers. They were magic to her.

'I'll call her,' muttered her kind-hearted older brother. James was gentle, helpful, handsome, athletic and above all brilliant. His parents were very proud of him. He was fourteen years old, and his sister Chichi was nine.

James liked science. He liked doing experiments with batteries and wires. He could take a radio set to bits — and put it together again. He also invented wonderful machines. Some of them worked. Most of them didn't.

His parents let him make his machines in the room where they kept boxes and suitcases. They hoped that one day he might be a famous inventor or an engineer.

James fetched Chichi from the field and they sat down with their parents for their evening meal.

Afterwards, Chichi followed her brother into the box-room. She saw he was working on a fantastic machine.

'What's that?' she asked.

'It's a three-dimensional enlarger,' he said proudly.

'A what?'

'It makes things larger.'

'Like enlarging a photocopy?' asked Chichi.

'Yes, but this machine doesn't just make a larger copy of something. It actually makes the thing itself bigger. Something three-dimensional.'

Chichi knew about three-dimensional things. 'Like this kola nut,' she said, picking it up. 'It's not just flat — long and wide. It's thick as well.'

James took the kola nut and put it in the machine. Then he switched on the light. Chichi was amazed. It really worked! The real circumference of the nut was about 8 cm, but under the machine it was about 24 cm round.

She gave the giant kola nut a push. It rolled out of the enlarger onto the table. It still kept its giant size.

'Isn't this a rather important invention?' she asked.

'It might be — and it also makes things smaller. You just turn this handle the other way. Like this . . . '

James put a book under the light and turned the handle. The book became so small that the print was impossible to read.

'It's an *ensmaller*, too!' Chichi laughed.

'It's a bit dangerous,' James said. 'If someone's hand got underneath, it might make it small, too.' Chichi shuddered at the thought. 'So you mustn't let anyone see or touch the machine.'

But the next day, when Chichi's friend Sara came to play, Chichi showed her the machine. She was explaining how it worked when Sara turned the handle. Immediately, Chichi disappeared. Sara was puzzled. 'Where has she gone?' she wondered. She ran downstairs to the kitchen.

'Please, have you seen Chichi?' she asked. James was walking past the kitchen and heard the conversation. He realised at once what was wrong. For the first time in his life he was afraid to tell the truth. He dared not tell his mother that Chichi was now probably no bigger than a cockroach.

'I think she went that way,' he said to Sara. Sara
skipped off to find her friend and James ran upstairs and
burst into the box-room. Then he stopped. 'If I put my foot
on her, I'll squash her,' he thought. 'Oh, what a terrible
problem!' He got down on his knees and started to look
for his sister. After about five minutes he saw a little
creature waving its arms about. It was Chichi. She was
looking at a mouse hole.

'Chichi!' shouted James. 'Come away from that hole! A mouse will be like a monster to you! Oh, Chichi, I'm so sorry.' He picked her up, gently.

'Sorry?' What for?' squeaked Chichi in excitement. She did not sound anxious, or afraid. 'It's wonderful, being so small. Think what I can learn about insects now!'

James was horrified. 'What do you mean? Come on — I've got to get you back to the right size.'

'No,' said Chichi. 'I want you to carry me to the termite hill behind our house.'

'What?'

'I want to watch the termites.'

'Don't be stupid, Chichi,' said James. 'This is serious. You are only 2 cm tall. I must try to get you right at once.'

'I'll tell Mother about you.'

'What do you mean?' asked James.

'Mother will kill you if she finds out what your machine has done.'

'I know,' said James.

'Then you must do as I say. I want to watch the termites and find out how they live,' Chichi insisted.

'I can't,' said James. 'You'll get lost. You're so small. You're just one mouthful for a dog now. A mosquito bite will make you swell like a balloon!'

'Oh, James, don't change me back! I'll tell Mother and Father. Then they won't let you do experiments ever again.'

'I don't care,' said James. 'Your life is more important.'

'And they will be very, very angry,' said Chichi. 'Please, James, no one need know about it.'

'But it's nearly time to eat.'

'Tell them I have gone to Sara's house for lunch,' said Chichi.

'No.'

'Yes.'

James sighed, a long, lonely, miserable sigh. 'All right,' he said. 'But you've got to promise to meet me before the sun goes down.'

'I promise,' said Chichi. 'You are fantastic, James.'

'No, I'm not. The machine is fantastic. I'm scared. This is just awful.'

He carried her gently downstairs in one hand.

'I'm just going to the termi . . . er . . . to find Chichi,' he lied, as he walked past the kitchen.

'Thank you, James, you are a good son,' replied his mother.

James sighed. If she knew the truth! He carried Chichi to the termite hill and put her down.

'It's 12 noon,' he said.

'I know,' said Chichi. 'I have got my watch on.'

James looked. The watch strap was just a thread round the little girl's wrist and the face was no bigger than a seed.

'Can you read that?' he asked.

'Of course,' said Chichi. 'It looks normal to me.' She looked round. 'Goodness! What a mountain!'

'Mountain?' asked James. 'Oh, the termite hill. I suppose it does look like a mountain to you.' He sighed again, miserably. 'Will you change your mind?' he asked hopefully.

'Stop worrying. Go home to lunch and meet me here at 6 o'clock.'

'5.30,' said James.

'No — 6 o'clock,' said Chichi. 'I've got a lot to do.'

James stopped. 'Suppose the termites bite you?' he said.

'They won't,' said Chichi. 'Trust me.'

'I don't,' said James.

'Bye!'

James knelt, unhappily, near the hill and watched his very 'little' sister walk to a hole. The termites didn't seem to see her. He sat and watched until his mother called, then he walked slowly back to the house.

'Chichi is eating at Sara's house,' he said. His mother was busy pounding fufu. She did not hear the unhappiness in his voice.

'She has no right to go without asking me,' she grumbled, but she didn't say any more.

Chichi was excited. She still had her note-book and coloured pencils in her hand. She wanted to make some drawings of the termites.

Something opposite her moved. Chichi looked up. There, in front of her, was a termite with an enormous head. It looked very fierce. Suddenly it saw a small ant. In a second it grabbed the ant with its strong legs and jaws and crushed it to death.

'That's a soldier termite,' thought Chichi. Its big head was very hard, but its body was soft and weak. It didn't have any eyes.

'How did it know where the ant was?' Chichi wondered. 'Perhaps it can smell very well.' She began to draw the soldier termite in detail.

Just as she finished her drawing, another termite came up to the soldier. This one was different. It was not a soldier, because it did not have a big head. It was one of the millions of workers. It came up to the soldier termite and started to clean it. Then another worker came up to the soldier and offered it food.

'So! The soldiers can fight the ants and other enemies because they have big, hard heads, but they can't look after themselves,' Chichi thought. 'The workers have to feed them and clean them. I didn't know that!' Chichi made another drawing and wrote down some words next to it.

Chichi climbed further into the hole. It was very dark. It wasn't easy to see but she could just make out the many passages, and the chambers into which they opened. She stood still. There was a termite in front of her. It was dying. Immediately six workers, all of them small, blind and wingless, attacked it and ate it up.

'Ugh! They are cannibals,' she said to herself. 'But they have to keep their home clean and I suppose that's the only way.' She noticed there was no rubbish. The termites ate up or removed everything. She watched a worker eating up its fellow worker. She made a good drawing of it.

The worker's head was not nearly as big as the soldier's and its jaws were not as powerful. It was soft, white and totally blind.

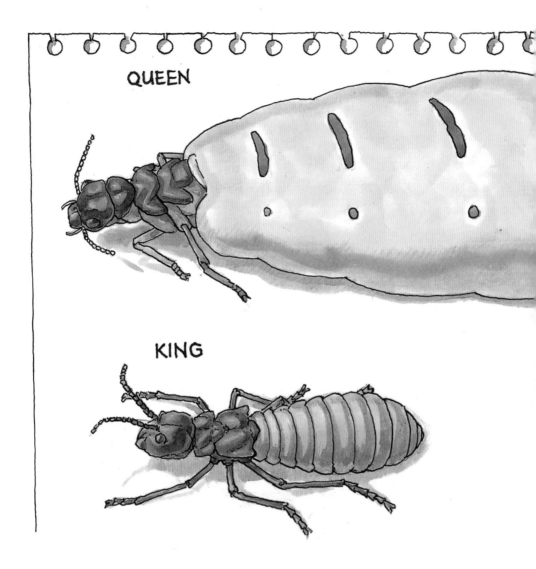

QUEEN

KING

As she walked on into another chamber, she accidentally broke off a piece of the wall. At once, a group of workers came to inspect it. They started to repair it. Chichi looked closely. They got little bits of soil and mixed it with the water from their mouths. This made a strong wall.

She walked on. It got darker and darker. Then she saw another chamber. There was a wall almost all the way round it. In the centre of that chamber she saw a huge termite which was very big and fat in the middle.

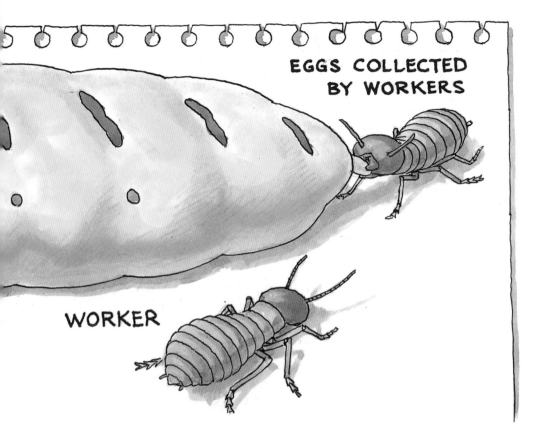

EGGS COLLECTED
BY WORKERS

WORKER

Chichi gasped. 'It's the queen. She's at least 8 cm long!'
Then she saw another termite next to the queen. This one
was darker in colour than the others, and much smaller
than the queen. It was the king. Chichi stood and watched.
The queen was laying a batch of eggs.

'I wonder what happens to them now,' thought
Chichi, but she didn't have to wonder for long. Soon a
group of workers came and started carrying the eggs
away.

She followed them. They went into a nearby
chamber. They put the eggs carefully in rows. Some older
eggs were already beginning to hatch. More workers were
coming in to feed the baby termites.

'There must be millions of workers,' she thought. 'But
I haven't seen many soldiers. I wonder why one termite is
born a soldier, and another is born a worker?'

Just then she saw another group of termites. They were bigger than the babies but they were not full size.

'Goodness! Their skins are splitting open!' she whispered, and she was right. 'I expect they have to change into a new skin when they grow and the old skin is too small.'

She walked on. She passed many chambers. In some chambers there were babies. In some chambers there were eggs. In others there were food stores. All around her, the termites worked.

Chichi thought about the big, fat, ugly white queen again. 'At least she doesn't have to work all day,' she thought. 'I think I'd rather be the queen than one of these poor workers. I wonder if they sleep at night?' Then she remembered the narrow passage which led to the queen's chamber. 'The queen's a prisoner!' she thought. 'How terrible! She can never get out of that chamber. She must stay there and lay eggs every day. I think I'd rather be a worker, busy all the time, but free to move around.'

Then Chichi had another thought. 'It's June. It's the time of the year when the marriage flight takes place.' Quickly she began to explore more and more little chambers. At last she found what she was looking for — thousands and thousands of termites, all with wings.

'Every year some of the termites grow wings and fly away,' she remembered. 'This must be the night. They are going to fly.' She looked at her watch. 5.30 pm. 'I've just got time to make a quick drawing of a winged termite.'

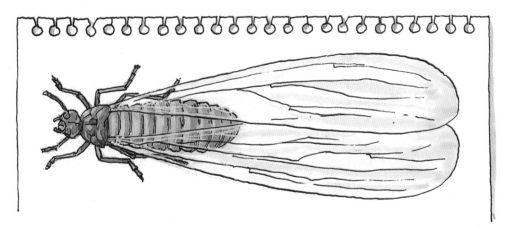

'Now I must go and meet James.' She looked around and started to walk towards the light. 'Termites hate light, because they are white,' she thought, 'but I'm beginning to miss it.'

Twenty minutes later she got out of the hill. She looked around.

The ground was very wet. 'There's been a storm,' she thought. 'Well, the rain didn't get into the termite hill.'

Suddenly, a great shadow swooped towards her. It was her brother's hand. He picked her up and held her close to his face.

'Thank goodness you're safe!' he said. 'Now I'm taking you home.'

'No, James, please wait a minute,' said Chichi. 'The termites are going to fly tonight. I want to watch their marriage flight.'

'Their what?' asked James.

Chichi explained. 'Just a few minutes, please!'

'No,' said James. 'We've got to get back. It's nearly time for the evening meal.'

'Please, James,' said Chichi. 'Remember, I can tell Mother about your machine.'

James groaned. He put Chichi down by one of the holes in the termite hill. Soon there was a rustling and a shaking. Chichi saw thousands of excited termites, all with wings, coming up out of the holes. She felt a movement beside her. Frogs and lizards were snapping up the termites as fast as they could. She looked up and saw birds flying around. They, too, were eating the termites. What a feast for them all!

Those termites which escaped flew only a few hundred metres. Then they landed and rubbed off their wings. They found a mate and went off to find a crack in the soft ground. They went into the crack, and made a little hole under the ground.

'They're going to make the first chamber of a new termite hill,' said Chichi.

'Satisfied?' asked James.

'Yes — that was wonderful,' replied Chichi.

On the way back to the house, she told him all about her adventure, but James was silent.

'What's the matter?' she asked.

'Suppose the machine doesn't work in reverse?' said James.

'Don't be silly, James,' said Chichi. 'You're a brilliant inventor. I know it will work.'

James sighed again. He was still afraid. His parents loved Chichi so much. So did he. What if . . . ?

'JAMES!' shouted his father as they reached the house.

'Yes, Father?'

'Go to Bai's house. They're selling chickens. I want you to buy two.'

'Just a minute, Father, I must . . . '

'When I say go, I mean now!' shouted his father. 'Not when you have finished playing with your stupid machines.'

'But . . . '

'JAMES!'

'Don't worry,' a little voice came from the palm of his hand. 'Just put me in your pocket. I'll be all right.'

'This day will never end,' groaned James. He set off for Bai's house, collected the chickens and returned.

At that moment everything went dark.

'Chichi,' whispered James, 'The electricity's off.'

'I know,' replied his sister. 'Just because I'm small it doesn't mean I can't see.'

'JAMES!' roared his father. 'Start the generator.'

'Yes, Father.' James went to the compound and started up the generator. Then his mother called.

'JAMES!'

'Yes, Mother?'

'Please fetch Chichi from Sara's house. I don't know why she has stayed so long.'

'I'm going,' said James, 'but I must get something from my room first.'

His father heard him. 'JAMES! Go at once or I'll smash every one of your stupid machines.'

'NO!' gasped James. He wanted to explain — or rush to Sara's house — or dash upstairs.

'I'm going.' He ran out of the door, hid behind the house, waited a minute, then returned.

'Chichi's on her way back from Sara's house,' he called to his mother. He tried to reach the stairs once more.

'ON HER WAY! Why isn't she with you?' His mother was getting angry.

'She's just . . . tidying the room . . . I want to check something upstairs . . . '

Now his father was angry too. 'JAMES! Wash your hands and sit down.'

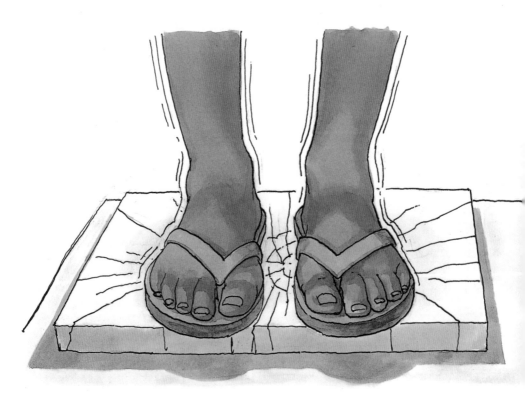

James didn't listen to his father but fled to the box-room. He placed Chichi on the glass plate, pushed her note-book into her hand, switched on the current — and prayed. Then he turned on the switch. The glass plate broke as Chichi returned to her normal size. There she was, smiling happily.

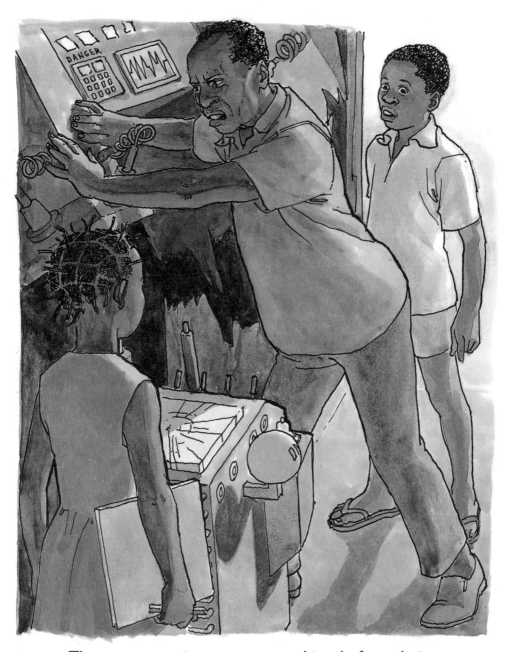

There was no time to say anything before their father came furiously into the room. He grabbed the machine and smashed it.

'Now get to bed, both of you,' he said. 'Next time you don't do what I say, I shall break your heads.'

James and Chichi fled.

'No supper for us tonight,' said James.

'I'm starving,' complained Chichi, 'And your machine's broken, James.'

'I don't care if I never see another machine,' said James, 'Oh, Chichi, I was so scared!'

'I wasn't,' said Chichi. 'I've got some marvellous drawings. Will you make me very small again one day? I want to go down a mouse hole!'

'Never, never, never!' said James, and they both laughed.

HOP STEP JUMP

In My Father's Village   Michael Palmer
Striped Paint   Rosina Umelo
The Slow Chameleon and **Shammy's Bride**   David Cobb
The Walking Talking Flying ABC   David Cobb

Choose Me!   Lynn Kramer
Nondo the Cow   Diane Rasteiro
Sika in the Snow   David Cobb

Chichi and the Termites   Wendy Ijioma
The Boy who ate a Hyena   James G D Ngumy
Tickets for the Zed Band   Lynn Kramer